For Jane and Lowdy – *J.D.*
For Rosamund Inglis – *G.P.*

First published in Great Britain in 1996 by
Frances Lincoln Limited, 4 Torriano Mews
Torriano Avenue, London NW5 2RZ

First paperback edition 1997

British Library Cataloguing in Publication Data
available on request

ISBN 0-7112-1023-3 hardback
ISBN 0-7112-1080-2 paperback

Printed in Hong Kong

1 3 5 7 9 8 6 4 2

Joyce Dunbar was born and brought up in Lincolnshire and for many years she worked in further education. She is an internationally acclaimed writer whose children's titles range from collections of short stories to *Mundo and the Weatherchild* (Heinemann), which was runner-up for the 1985 Guardian Children's Fiction Award, and the *Mouse and Mole* series (Transworld). *Indigo and the Whale* is Joyce Dunbar's first book for Frances Lincoln.

Geoffrey Patterson divides his time between Ipswich and the South of France. Formerly an interior designer and a set designer for the BBC, he is now a full-time author and illustrator of children's books. His previous titles for Frances Lincoln include *Jonah and the Whale*, *The Lion and the Gypsy*, which was nominated for the 1991 Kate Greenaway Medal, and *Stories from the Bible*, written by Martin Waddell.

INDIGO
AND THE
WHALE
JOYCE DUNBAR
Illustrated by
GEOFFREY PATTERSON

FRANCES LINCOLN

Once there was a boy whose eyes were so blue that his parents named him Indigo. His father was a fisherman, and every morning they went fishing together.

But Indigo wasn't much help to his father. He was too busy playing tunes on an ebony pipe he had found to bother about fishing.

In the evenings, his tame jackdaw loved to listen.

One day, when they were out in the boat, Indigo said to his father, "I don't want to be a fisherman. I'm no good at catching fish. I want to be a musician."

"Stupid boy!" said his father. "You can't earn a living playing tunes. You can't eat music!"

"But perhaps I could make music so wonderful that people would pay to listen to me," said the boy.

His father became angry at this. "I am a fisherman. My father was a fisherman. My father's father was a fisherman. You too shall be a fisherman!"

And with that, he snatched the ebony pipe from his son and threw it into the sea.

So Indigo could no longer play his tunes, and his jackdaw began to pine. Indigo offered him crumbs, but the jackdaw refused to take them.

"Play a tune on your ebony pipe," said the jackdaw. "Then I will want to eat."

"I can't," said Indigo. "My father has thrown it into the sea. He says I must be a fisherman like him."

Soon afterwards, Indigo's father fell ill and was unable to take out the boat.

"You will have to go alone," said Indigo's mother, "otherwise we will starve. Be sure to bring back a good catch."

When the jackdaw heard about this, he flew into the forest. He returned with a reed pipe that was all the colours of the rainbow. "This pipe has a special charm," he told Indigo. "Play it out at sea and bring back your catch, and you will never have to go fishing again."

"But I can't go fishing with a reed pipe," said Indigo.

"Oh yes you can," said the jackdaw, "though you may not be fishing for fish!"

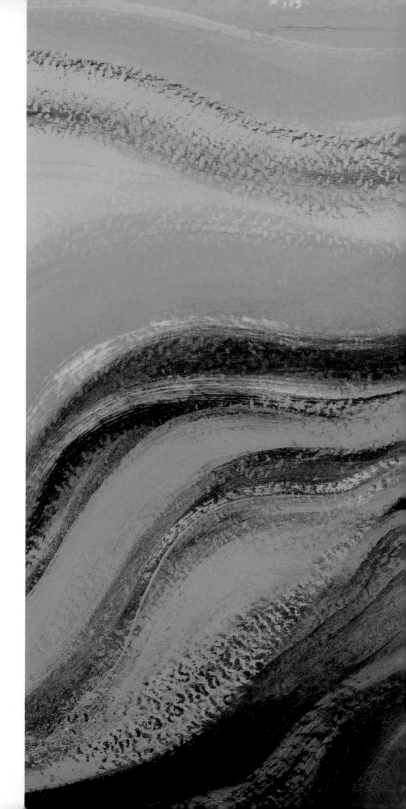

So Indigo followed the jackdaw's advice. He took
the boat out on his own and when he was far out
at sea he began to play a tune.

A strange shadow appeared underwater. While
Indigo played, his boat began to surge through the
waves as if carried along by strong currents.

Suddenly, a great creature broke the surface.
It wasn't a fish at all: Indigo had charmed a whale!

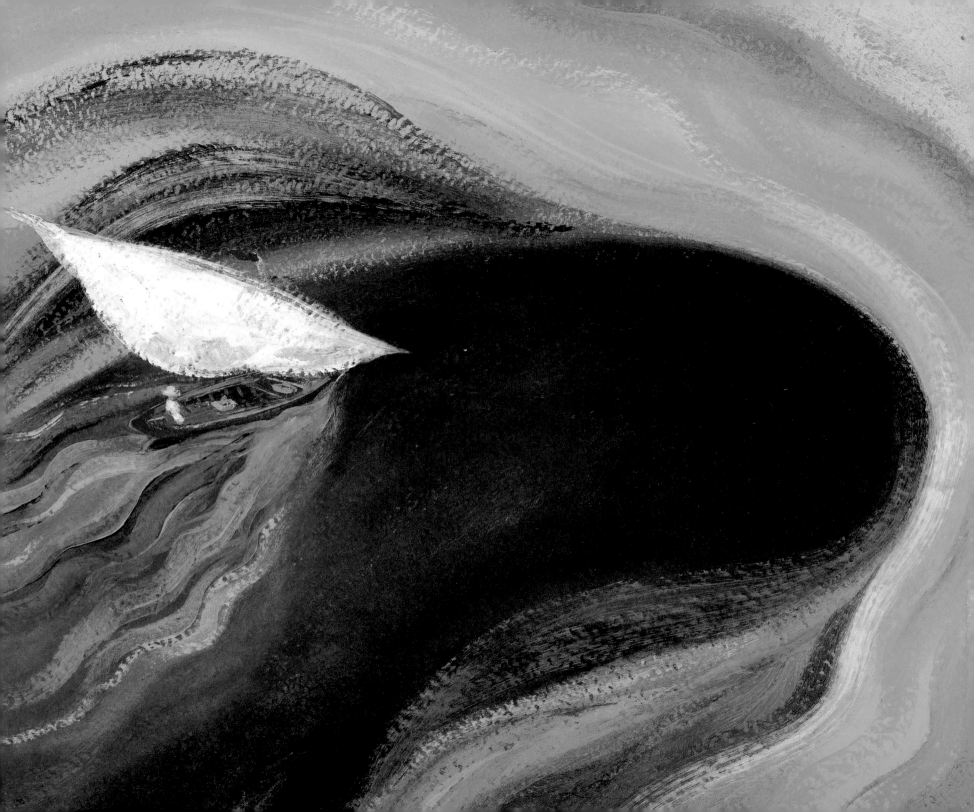

"Please stop your playing," said the whale.

"I won't," said Indigo. "My father is ill and I dare not return without a catch. I must charm you back to the shore."

But when he put the pipe back to his lips, the whale dived under the water.

A deep, strange sound began. The whale was singing
her song. Another whale answered, then another, so that
Indigo's pipe could hardly be heard. Instead, it was his
boat that was charmed, pulled along by the sound.

The whale sang and swam, sang and swam, pulling
the boat along, until they came to a place where
the land was white and the sea was icy cold. Indigo
shivered and his teeth chattered so much that he
thought he would freeze to death.

"Now will you stop your playing?" said the whale.

"No," murmured Indigo, "I will not."

Then the whale began to sing a different song.
Another whale answered, then another. Once more,
the boat was pulled along. This time they came to a place
where the land was parched and dry and the sea was
burning hot. Indigo thought he would die of thirst.

"Now will you stop your playing?" said the whale.
"No," panted Indigo, "I will not."

The whale began yet a third song. Other whales answered. The boat was pulled to the bottom of the ocean, to its dark, cavernous depths, so that Indigo could neither see nor breathe. He thought he was going to drown.

"Now will you stop your playing?" said the whale.

"No," gasped Indigo. "I will not."

At this, the whale gave a deep sigh and all the singing stopped.
Indigo and his boat shot to the surface of the water. Although
the whale was so big, she could no longer resist the charm
of the rainbow pipe and she followed Indigo back to the shore.

The whale made the saddest sound and it seemed that all
the whales were weeping.

"I'm sorry," said Indigo, "but my mother will be so pleased
if I take you back to my village. And I will never have to fish again.
I will be able to make music instead."

Then utter silence fell and something strange began to happen. As the life drained out of the whale, so the colours all around began to fade, until Indigo stood in a world where everything was grey. Even Indigo's eyes were grey, which had always been so blue.

And the world stayed utterly silent.

Indigo felt pity for the whale. He could see no joy in his music if the whale could no longer make hers. He could feel no pride in such a catch.

"I will stop my playing," he murmured, and he broke the rainbow pipe into pieces.

No sooner had he done this than a great wave rolled up to the shore and carried the whale back out to sea. She began to sing and swim, and all the other whales sang with her. They sang back the colours of the world.

It was the most wonderful music that Indigo had ever heard.

Then Indigo saw something at his feet. It was his precious ebony pipe!

Indigo went back to his village. His jackdaw was the first to greet him.

"Now will you play me a tune?" asked the jackdaw. So Indigo put the pipe to his lips and began to play the whale music.

Everyone came to listen. They had never heard such music before, that was filled with the colours of the world. "Play us some more," they begged.

Indigo's father listened too, and his spirits were immediately restored.

"Where did you find such music?" he asked his son.

"At sea, father," answered the boy.

Indigo's father smiled. "I am a fisherman," he said, "my father was a fisherman, and my father's father was a fisherman. But my son - *he* is a musician!"

MORE PICTURE BOOKS IN PAPERBACK FROM FRANCES LINCOLN

CAMILLE AND THE SUNFLOWERS
Laurence Anholt

"One day a strange man arrived in Camille's town. He had a straw hat and a yellow beard..."   The strange man is the artist Vincent van Gogh, seen through the eyes of a young boy entranced by Vincent's painting. An enchanting introduction to the great painter, with reproductions of Van Gogh's work.

Suitable for National Curriculum English - Reading, Key Stage 1
Art - Knowledge and Understanding, Key Stage 2
Scottish Guidelines, English Language - Reading, Levels A and B
ISBN 0-7112-1050-0   £4.99

LITTLE INCHKIN
Fiona French

Little Inchkin is only as big as a lotus flower, but he has the courage of a Samurai warrior. How he proves his valour, wins the hand of a princess, and is granted his dearest wish by the Lord Buddha is charmingly retold in this Tom Thumb legend of old Japan.

Suitable for National Curriculum English - Reading, Key Stages 1 and 2
Scottish Guidelines, English Language - Reading, Levels A and B
ISBN 0-7112-0917-0   £4.99

CHINYE
Obi Onyefulu
Illustrated by Evie Safarewicz

Poor Chinye! Back and forth through the forest she goes, fetching and carrying for her cruel stepmother. But strange powers are watching over her, and soon her life will be magically transformed... An enchanting retelling of a traditional West African folk tale of goodness, greed and a treasure-house of gold.

Suitable for National Curriculum English - Reading, Key Stages 1 and 2
Scottish Guidelines, English Language - Reading, Level B
ISBN 0-7112-1052-7   £4.99

All Frances Lincoln titles are available at your local bookshop or by post from:
Frances Lincoln Books, B.B.C.S., P.O. Box 941, Hull, North Humberside, HU1 3YQ.
24 Hour Credit Card Line 01482 224626
To order, send:
Title, author, ISBN number and price for each book ordered.
Your full name and address.
Cheque or postal order made payable to B.B.C.S.
for the total amount, plus postage and packing as below.
U.K. & B.F.P.O. - £1.00 for the first book,
and 50p for each additional book up to a maximum of £3.50.
Overseas & Eire - £2.00 for the first book, £1.00 for the second
and 50p for each additional book.

Prices and availability are subject to change without notice.